Namaste!

Namaste (pronounced *nah-mah-stay*) literally means "I bow to you."
It is generally translated as "the light in me meets the light in you."

DEDICATION

To Sir Edmund Hillary and Tenzing Norgay

*To my goddaughter Juliette Allayaud, and for those who practice an understanding of "namaste"
everyday in their relations with others and in their teachings –Peggy Orr, Nikki Estrada, Lisa
Schubert, Kewulay Kamara, Gene Gollogly, Paul Winter, and Kevin and Erin Maile O'Keefe –
and to my extended family in Kathmandu, Nepal – Anjana, Purna, Prajwol, and Siddhartha Shakya
– and for Ellen Coon and Ted Riccardi who introduced me to this special part of the world. – D.C.*

To all those who helped make NAMASTE! *come into being, and to loving kindness – may it find
its home in each and every heart in this our one, precious world. – A.C.*

*To the memories of my father-in-law, Mr. Pasang Kami (PK) Sherpa and to my father,
Mr. Mingma Tsering Sherpa, whose lives have been an inspiration to me and my family
and have provided me with incredible support. –A.R.S.*

Text © 2009 by Diana Cohn.
Illustrations © 2009 by Amy Córdova.

The illustrations in this book were rendered in acrylic on a gessoed ground with colored pencil.

ISBN 978-162148-005-1

SteinerBooks
610 Main Street Great Barrington, MA 01230

www.steinerbooks.org

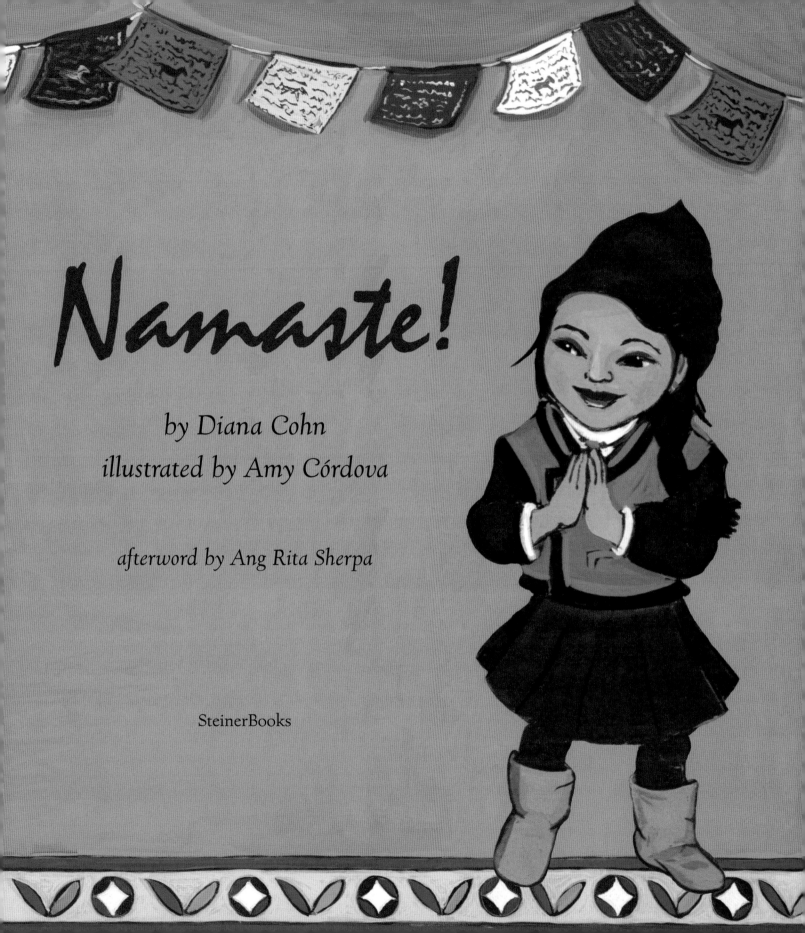

Namaste!

by Diana Cohn

illustrated by Amy Córdova

afterword by Ang Rita Sherpa

SteinerBooks

nima Sherpa lives at the top of the world, where the tallest
mountain on earth, Chomolongma, towers above the clouds,

On the roof of Nima's house, yellow, green, red, white, and blue prayer flags flutter and flap in the early morning winds. Down the hillside the Milk River rushes, white with cold.

Every year, Nima's father leaves home to work as a mountain guide.
Although he is gone just a few weeks, for Nima it feels as if a whole

year passes before he returns. While he is away, Nima misses her father's stories of the magical mountains of Nepal.

For breakfast, Nima's mother makes tsampa, a porridge of roasted barley mixed with yak butter tea. "Nima," her father says, as they eat together, "when I come home, I will have a story for you, as I always do.

Nima and her mother light some incense and offer blessings for her
father's journey. Although he always knows when a storm is coming,

even before the dark clouds begin to gather, and he never gets lost,
Nima prays to the tiger-riding goddess to keep her father safe.

Nima's father will help travelers who come from all over the world to walk through the Himalayas and see Chomolongma – the mountain they call Everest. One day Nima hopes to join her father on one of his treks,

Before he sets off, Nima's father prays as he tosses a handful of rice toward the mountains. Nima's mother gently places a khata around his neck for good luck.

Then Nima gets ready for the long walk to the market village where she goes
to school. Every day, she passes dozens of people on her way. When she sees
them, she brings her hands together with her fingers almost touching her chin

bows her head slightly, and says *Namaste!* "*Namaste* means *the light in me meets the light in you*," Nima's mother tells her. "When you say *Namaste!* try

As Nima walks along, she meets some porters carrying big baskets of biscuits and tea and pots and pans of all sizes. She remembers her father's stories about helping people. Maybe the story she will tell him will be about how she helps others, too.

But Nima is too little to carry such a heavy load. Can she find another way to help them? Nima calls out *Namaste!* The porters are very tired, but when

Soon Nima hears a silvery *ching-sing-sing*, *ching-sing-sing* behind her.
The bells ring and ring from a caravan of yaks and naks that weaves

Nima waits patiently at the side of the dusty road. *Namaste!* she says
quietly to her animal friends as they clamor past.

As Nima skips along, she sees a group of travelers looking at a stupa by the side of the road. She wonders how she can help them? She doesn't

The travelers smile at Nima, and bring their hands together and bow their heads, just as she does. *Namaste!* they all say together.

After school, Nima sees her father's friend Tenzing, a Tibetan trader. He is sitting in the marketplace among the other traders who have walked many weeks over the high mountains to sell and trade salt and butter, jewelry and fabrics, and other wares. Tenzing trades his carved bone bowls for some jars filled with honey. *Namaste!* Nima shouts. Tenzing's smile breaks across his broad face like the rays of the sun streaming through a cloud. *Namaste!* he says

Tenzing motions for Nima to sit beside him and offers her a spoonful of the golden honey. "Nima, you are full of sweetness and light, just like this honey." Nima smiles at her old friend. "Thank you, Tenzing," she says.

savoring the treat. "And," says Tenzing, "you brighten my day every
time you share that sweetness and light, every time you say *Namaste!*"

On her way home, Nima shares her sweetness and light with every *Namaste!* she says   with monks on their way to their monasteries   with porters

Nima will have a story for her father when he returns home.
She will tell him how she helps others every time she says *Namaste!*

The light in me

meets the light in you.

GLOSSARY

Chomolongma – is the Tibetan and Sherpa name for the tallest mountain in the world. It means "Mother Goddess of the Earth." In the Nepali language, it is called "Sagarmatha," which means "forehead in the sky." In the West this mountain is well known as Mount Everest.

Khata – is a ceremonial cloth that is draped around a person's neck like a scarf, and is given as an offering and for good luck. It is often presented as a gift at festive occasions. Khatas are usually made of white or yellow silk.

Namaste – (pronounced *nah-mah-stay*) literally means "I bow to you." It is generally translated as "the light in me meets the light in you." When spoken to another person, it is commonly accompanied by a slight bow. The gesture is made with the hands pressed together, palms touching and fingers pointed upward, in front of the chest. The greeting *Namaste* represents the belief that there is a Divine spark within each of us. The gesture without words carries the same meaning.

Nima – means "Sun." It is traditional for the Sherpas to give a child the name of the day on which he or she was born, and so Nima's name indicates that she was born on a Sunday.

Prayer flags – Tibetans consider prayer flags to be holy. Prayer flags are hung in the open – outside temples and holy sites, strung across bridges, rooftops, and mountain passes – where the flags can meet the wind. The Tibetans believe that when the flags are blown by the wind, the prayers printed on the flags will spread good will, peace, and compassion to all. The five colors of the prayer flags represent the elements:

Blue	–	sky/space
White	–	air/wind
Red	–	fire
Green	–	water
Yellow	–	earth

Sherpa – means "people from the east." Sherpas are an ethnic group who live in Nepal and are known worldwide for their great skill as mountain climbers, guides, and traders.

Stupa – A mound-like structure that contains holy objects or relics. It is one of the most ancient forms of Buddhist art. Stupas are the most numerous monuments in Buddhist areas and are designed with deep symbolism and sacred geometry to emanate blessings and peace.

Tenzing – is a common Tibetan name that means "holder of the teachings" or "bearer of wisdom."

Tiger-riding goddess – The Tibetans believe that their mountains are sacred and are protected by gods and goddesses. Chomolongma is protected by Jomo Miyo-Lang-Sangma, a goddess often depicted riding on a tiger and holding a bowl of tsampa.

Tsampa – This porridge made from barley flour and mixed with salty, yak butter tea is a staple food in Sherpa households.

Yak and nak (male and female of the species) – These high altitude animals provide hide for leather, milk for dairy products, meat, wool for clothing, and dung for fuel and fertilizer. Tibetan traders use these animals to carry products from village to village, transporting their goods over great distances and high mountain passes.

AFTERWORD
by Ang Rita Sherpa

NEPAL

About 29 million people live in Nepal. Although Nepali is the official language, most of the ethnic groups who live in the different regions of this country have their own languages, lifestyles, and customs. Religion is a deeply rooted part of Nepali life. Hinduism is the primary religion, but Buddhism and other beliefs are interwoven with many of the traditions and festivals that permeate every aspect of life in this country.

Nepal is rectangular in shape. Three geographic regions – Terai, Mountain, and Hill – run its length in three belts, corresponding roughly to elevation, from low in the south to high in the north. The Terai, in the south, is home to jungles with tigers, rhinoceroses, and elephants. The Mountain region in the north includes the Himalayas.

THE HIMALAYAS

The world's highest mountains are located in Asia. The Himalaya Mountain Range is still rising, and its peaks have not yet been worn down as have older mountain chains. Eight of the tallest mountains in the world are part of the Himalayas: Everest, Kanchenjunga, Lhotse, Makalu, Cho Oyu, Dhanlagiri, Manaslu, and Annapurna.

This area is refuge for many threatened and endangered wildlife species, including the snow leopard, musk deer, red panda, and Himalayan black bear. Scores of rhododendron and orchid species are visited by over 300 bird species.

THE SHERPA PEOPLE

The Sherpas are Nepal's best-known ethnic group. Bringing their Tibetan Buddhist traditions and culture, they migrated from eastern Tibet and settled in the rugged mountain valleys in the Khumbu region of northeastern Nepal over 500 years ago.

Sherpa food is limited to crops that can grow at high altitudes. Potatoes, buckwheat, and barley are the traditional main foods in the Khumbu region. Sherpas also grow turnips and greens and make dairy products such as butter, yogurt and cheese from the milk of their yaks. Tibetan traders travel with yak caravans over the high passes of the Himalayas to sell salt and dried meat in the Sherpa markets.

SIR EDMUND HILLARY AND TENZING NORGAY

On May 29, 1953, the New Zealand mountaineer Sir Edmund Hillary along with mountaineer Sherpa Tenzing Norgay became the first climbers to reach the summit of Mount Everest. Following his ascent of Everest, Sir Edmund founded the Himalayan Trust and devoted much of the rest of his life to helping the Sherpa people of Nepal. Through his efforts many schools and hospitals were built in the Solo Khumbu region of the Himalayas.

The accomplishment of climbing Mount Everest inspired many visitors to come see the tallest mountain in the world. Rising tourism brought new jobs and opportunities for the Sherpa people, but also has had a damaging impact on this remote and fragile environment. Thanks to the work of Sir Edmund and others, in 1976 Sagarmatha National Park was established to protect this very special place. In 1979, the region was declared a World Heritage Natural Site in recognition of its unique ecology and the cultural heritage of the Sherpa people.

PRESERVING MOUNTAIN CULTURES

Many people and organizations care deeply for this part of the world and are dedicated to safeguarding its beauty and cultures. One organization working to preserve mountain cultures all over the world, including in the Himalayan region, is The Mountain Institute (TMI), founded in 1972. Based in Washington, DC, The Mountain Institute has offices and community-based programs in the Andean and Appalachian mountain ranges, as well as the Himalayan mountain range. Their goal is to empower communities living in some of the world's most remote and rugged regions to protect their environments while enhancing their livelihoods.

Mountain people themselves live close to the land, and their farming, grazing, hunting and woodcutting maintain a delicate balance between sustainability and destruction. But mountains, often in the world's "hot spots" of biodiversity, are rich in timber, water, and mineral resources that attract severe development pressures to fragile areas. The growing lure and accessibility of mountains as tourist destinations also places strains on infrastructure and ecosystems. To minimize these effects, TMI works in partnership with other organizations to create effective means of conserving the unique mountain ecosystems and species.

Amy Córdova, Ang Rita Sherpa, Diana Cohn

Diana Cohn is an award-winning children's book author. For over two decades she has worked on environmental, economic, and global justice issues as a teacher, media activist, and program director for foundations with social change philanthropy missions. Her books include *Roses for Isabella; Dream Carver; Si Se Puede! Yes We Can! Janitor Strike in LA; Mr. Goethe's Garden;* and *The Bee Tree*. Diana lives with her husband in northern California.

Amy Córdova is art educator and artist, whose art reflects soul and spirit. She has been recognized for her work as an illustrator of children's books, including the Wisconsin Library Award and twice honor winner of the American Library Association's Pura Belpré Award. Amy lives in Santa Fe, New Mexico.

Ang Rita Sherpa is Senior Program Manager for The Mountain Institute Himal Program. He has a master's degree in Protected Landscape Management from the University of Wales, UK.

*　*　*　*

The author and illustrator of this book witnessed the work of The Mountain Institute while doing research for their book in Nepal. With deeply felt gratitude for the generosity of The Mountain Institute staff in Kathmandu, they are donating a portion of the proceeds from the sale of Namaste! to support the Institute's critical work preserving mountain cultures in the Himalayas and around the world.